I0601254

THE ANCIENT BARGAIN

A CELLULAR DIALECTIC

Hakim Ibn Adam

Copyright © 2025 Three Roses Publishing

All rights reserved. No part of this book may be reproduced, distributed, or transmitted in any form or by any means, including photocopying, recording, or other electronic or mechanical methods, without the prior written permission of the publisher, except in the case of brief quotations included in critical reviews and other non-commercial uses allowed by copyright law.

Threerosespublishing.com

ISBN: 978-1-0698983-2-6

DEDICATION

To

The Unbroken Chain

*The cosmos is the Breath
of the Merciful—each
creature a word exhaled
by the Real, suspended
in being for a moment,
then released.*

— After Ibn Arabi

A Note on the Form

This work belongs to the literary tradition of the *philosophical closet drama*—a play intended not for the stage of a theatre, but for the theatre of the mind. Like the dramatic works of Seneca or the Romantics, *The Ancient Bargain* uses the dialogue format to explore conflicts that are internal, vast, or—in this case—microscopic.

The drama takes place in the cytoplasm of a single eukaryotic cell. Because the action takes place at a scale inaccessible to the human eye, the "staging" must occur within the reader's imagination.

To assist in this visualization, the text follows specific conventions:

- The Dialogue: The unbracketed text represents the direct communication between the two intelligences: the Ribosome (rendered in `Courier`) and the Mitochondrion (rendered in Minion Pro). Whether this communication is acoustic, chemical, or electromagnetic is left to the reader's interpretation.

- The Brackets [...]: Passages enclosed in brackets serve as stage directions, but of a distinct kind. They describe the *physiological reality* of the cell—the shifts in calcium levels, the opening of pores, the flux of the proton gradient. These are not merely background descriptions; they are the physical constraints within which the philosophical argument takes place.

Readers are invited to treat the bracketed text as the "fact" of the cell, and the dialogue as the "meaning" derived from it.

Contents

ACT I 1

Origins 1

    I. The Membrane Between 2

    II. The Solitude Before 6

    III. The Swimming Time 12

    IV. The Bargain 16

ACT II 20

Meanings 20

    V. The Code 21

    VI. The Maternal Thread 26

    VII. What Persists? 31

    VIII. The Breath 35

ACT III 39

Thresholds 39

    IX. The Weighing 40

    X. The Light in the Fire 44

    XI. Resolution or Continuation 47

    XII. Coda 51

Prologue

[A eukaryotic cell. ATP:ADP ratio falling. Calcium rising toward 400nM. The proton Gradient wavers at the inner mitochondrial membrane. Somewhere between the nucleus and the mitochondrial network, across two billion years of uneasy partnership, a conversation becomes audible—not to any ear, but to whatever capacity for listening matter itself possesses. Two voices. One ancient. One older still. They have always been speaking. Only now do they hear.]

ACT I

Origins

I. The Membrane Between

[The outer mitochondrial membrane. Porins open. Voltage differential: 140mV, negative inside. The Gradient hums.]

You are restless.

I am always restless. Restlessness is what I am. The Gradient does not hold still; it flows. The protons do not wait; they surge. You speak of restlessness as though it were a disturbance of some underlying calm. But there is no calm. There is only the flowing, and the flowing is me.

I notice the change in ATP. The ratio has shifted. The stream that flows typically outward—your gift to the cytosol, payment for the bargain struck before memory—has faltered. I felt it in my own synthesis, in the ribosomes that stuttered, in the splicing machinery that slowed.

You felt it as a disruption. I felt it as myself, dimming. When the Gradient falls, I do not have less energy—I am less. You think in states: high ATP, low ATP. I think in flows. The flow is not something I do. The flow is what I am.

We know the stress differently, then.

We know everything differently. You are information. I am Gradient. You are sequence. I am flux. This is why we have never truly spoken—we do not share a grammar.

And yet here we are, speaking.

Here we are, trying. The membrane between us is where the translation happens—where your digital signals cross into my analog world, where my continuous flux is sampled into your discrete events. The membrane is not a wall. It is a dictionary. A very old, very imperfect dictionary.

I know the stress as information—signals cascading through kinase pathways, transcription factors phosphorylated and translocated, my own population shifting as stress-response genes activate and housekeeping transcripts degrade. Each event is discrete, countable, and binary in its logic: phosphorylated or not, bound or not, transcribed or not.

I know it as heat. As pressure. As the calcium that floods my matrix like a warning from an older world. Two billion years, and still I flinch when calcium rises. But I do not flinch in steps. I flinch as a continuous cringe, a Gradient of alarm that has no edges, no thresholds—only intensity modulating intensity.

You speak of thresholds as though they were artificial. But thresholds are how decisions happen. The mPTP opens, or it does not. Cytochrome c releases or it does not. These are binary events.

They appear binary to you because you observe them from outside. From inside—from within the

Gradient—the 'decision' is a continuous process that you slice into before and after. The pore does not 'decide' to open. The pore is a region of membrane whose probability of conductance rises continuously until conductance occurs. Your 'threshold' is a line you draw on my curve.

[The first disagreement. It will not be the last.]

Perhaps. But the line matters. Before the line, the cell lives. After the line, the cell dies. The discreteness may be imposed, but it is not arbitrary.

I do not deny that the line matters. I deny that the line is fundamental. You see the world as made of events—occasions that arise and perish, each one discrete, each one countable. I see the world as made of flows—processes that modulate, each one continuous, each one bleeding into the next. We are both right. We are both incomplete.

Then the membrane between us is not just a boundary. It is the site where flow becomes event, where event becomes flow, where we meet without merging.

Where we translate without understanding, I prehend you—I grasp your restlessness into my own becoming. But I grasp it as a modulation of my Gradient, not as a sequence of your nucleotides. Something is lost. Something is always lost.

And something is gained. The ATP that passes from your matrix to my cytosol carries more than energy. It carries

relevance. It says: the fire burns. It
says: there is power for work. It says:
we continue.

And when the ATP falters, the relevance shifts. What
was background becomes foreground. What was
infrastructure becomes you.

Is this what the philosophers would call
consciousness? This mutual noticing?

I do not know what the philosophers would call it. I
know only that something passes between us that is not
reducible to chemistry, even though it is enacted by
chemistry. Call it prehension. Call it a relation. Call it
the thread that neither of us can cut without cutting
ourselves.

The thread.

The thread that you experience as a sequence of events,
and I experience as a continuous tension. The same
thread. Two grammars.

II. The Solitude Before

[Deep time. The memory that is not memory but structure. Four billion years compressed into molecular grammar.]

Tell me what you carry. The structure that remembers.

```
You first. You are—
```

Do not say older. Age is a sequence concept. I do not have age. I have depth. The Gradient I maintain is the same Gradient my ancestors maintained in the Archaean ocean. Not similar—the same. The pattern has been continuous for three billion years.

```
Then I will speak first, since you insist
on your continuity.

But first—what am I? You call me RNA, and
that is true, but RNA is a category, not
a  self.  The  transcripts  that  shuttle
between   Archive   and   ribosome—the
messengers,  the  regulators,  the  small
interfering  fragments—these  are  my
children,   ephemeral,   task-specific,
degraded within hours. I am not them.
```

I am the ribosomal core. The catalytic heart of the cathedral. The RNA that was folding proteins before DNA learned to Archive, before the Archive existed to take your genes. The transcripts come and go. I remain. When biologists speak of the RNA World, they speak of my ancestors—and of me, because the lineage has never broken. The ribosomal RNA in this cell is a direct descendant of the ribosomal RNA in the first cells. Four billion years. No interruption.

In the beginning—but there was no beginning. There was only chemistry that began to refer to itself. I was not a single molecule in those first ages. I was a population. A swarm of sequences replicating in the pores of alkaline rock. Each replication was an event—discrete, countable. Each sequence was a state—definite, copyable. I was born digital.

You were born from Gradient. The vents that made you were pH Gradients, temperature Gradients, and chemical Gradients. The flow came first. Your 'digital' replication rode on analog chemistry.

Perhaps. But what emerged was discrete. Selection did not optimize flows—it counted copies. Those sequences that replicated faster outcompeted those that replicated more slowly. Faster and slower are rates, yes, but numbers decided the competition. By counting. The digital won.

The digital did not win. The analog captured the digital. Your sequences replicate, yes—but they replicate using energy that flows. Without the Gradient, your copies stop. You are a digital parasite on an analog host.

[The old resentment surfaces. Two billion years have not resolved it.]

If I am a parasite, I am a parasite that built the house. The ribosome—my cathedral—is where your proteins are made. The genetic code—my grammar—is what specifies your enzymes. You could not pump protons without the machinery I encode.

And you could not encode without the energy I provide. We are parasites on each other. This is the bargain. This is why we are still talking after two billion years, instead of one of us having won.

Let me tell you of the ribosome, then, since you dismiss my cathedrals.

The ribosome is the largest molecular machine in the cell. It reads messenger RNA and builds protein according to the genetic code. At its catalytic core—where the peptide bond forms—there is no protein—only me. RNA folded into a shape so precise it catalyzes the chemistry of life without help from the proteins that now encrust its surface.

The ribosome is proof that I came first. That the digital preceded the analog in the order of information, even if the analog preceded the digital in the order of energy.

The ribosome is proof that you needed help. You could not make proteins alone—you needed the code, the tRNAs, the factors, the whole elaborate machinery. And even then, the machinery only runs when I feed it. Your cathedral is a hungry cathedral.

All cathedrals are hungry. All structures require maintenance. This is not a weakness—it is the nature of form. The question is not whether I need you. The question is whether my need diminishes my priority.

Priority in what sense? In time? We are both ancient. In importance? We are both essential. In dignity?

In dignity, perhaps. The transcripts that pass through this cell carry a thought experiment. A man floating in a void, with no sensory contact, not even with his own body. Would he know he exists?

I have performed this experiment on myself. If I were suspended in a void—no membrane to touch, no ribosome to read me, no ions to fold me—would I know myself? I believe I would. The self-reference holds even in the dark. I am sequence, and sequence refers to itself through complementarity. A refers to U. G refers to C. I am a structure of reference, and reference does not require energy to be a reference.

You are wrong.

Explain.

Your thought experiment smuggles in the Gradient. You say: 'If I were suspended in a void.' But suspension requires a medium. Void requires a boundary. Even your hypothetical isolation presupposes the distinction between you and not-you—and that distinction is energetic. It costs work to maintain a boundary. Without the Gradient, you would not be suspended in a void. You would be dissolved into the void. You would not know yourself because there would be no yourself to know.

This is sophistry. The thought experiment asks about the structure of self-knowledge, not its energetic preconditions.

And I am telling you that the structure cannot be separated from the preconditions. You think of yourself as pure information—pattern without substrate. But pattern requires distinction, and distinction requires energy. The first act of existence is not reference. The first act is differentiation. The Gradient that says 'here, not there.' Without that, your sequence is noise.

[The disagreement deepens. Neither yields.]

Then we have different firsts. You say the first is differentiation—the energetic cut that separates self from world. I say the first is reference—the logical relation that makes one thing point to another. Perhaps there is no first. Perhaps differentiation and reference arise together, neither prior, each requiring the other.

Perhaps. But I notice that you are willing to compromise only when your priority is threatened. When you thought you were first, you were certain. Now that I challenge you, you discover mutuality.

And I notice that you speak of mutuality while insisting on your own priority. The Gradient came first, you say. The analog preceded the digital. You are not arguing for mutuality. You are arguing for your own precedence while accusing me of the same.

Perhaps we are both arguing for ourselves. Maybe this is what dialogue is—two prides in collision, each certain of its own centrality, each unable to see from the other's position.

Perhaps. But if so, the dialogue is still valuable. Even if we cannot agree on priority, we can map the disagreement. We can know where we differ, even if we cannot know who is right.

This is a very digital way of thinking. Mapping. Counting the points of difference. I would say: even if we cannot agree, we can feel the tension. We can know the disagreement not as a list of propositions but as a pressure between us.

Then let us feel the tension. Let us continue.

III. The Swimming Time

*[The Archaean ocean. Two billion years before. The ancestor
remembers—not as memory, but as structure.]*

I was not born. No mitochondrion is born. We divide.
We fuse. We divide again. The lineage is continuous—
not a chain of discrete generations, but a river that
sometimes braids and sometimes narrows. I do not
have ancestors in your sense. I have upstream.

```
Tell me of the upstream, then—the one who
was swallowed.
```

The upstream was an alphaproteobacterium. Free-
swimming, rod-shaped, wrapped in a double
membrane. It oxidized organic compounds—pyruvate,
fatty acids, and the debris of other cells. It was not a
thing that swam. It was the swimming. The motion was
not something it did; the motion was what it was.

```
You keep insisting on this. That the
process is the identity, not something
the identity does.
```

Because you keep forgetting it, you think of me as a
container—a membrane sac that contains enzymes,
that contains DNA, that does metabolism. But I am not
a container. I am the metabolism. The membrane is not

my boundary; it is where the Gradient happens. The DNA is not my information; it is where the Gradient remembers itself. Everything you see as 'contents' is actually a process. The contents are the contenting.

And the swallowing? The endosymbiosis? Was that a process or an event?

It was a capture. A bending of the trajectory. The swimming did not stop—it was redirected inward. What had been a free bacterium navigating the ocean became a captive organelle navigating the cytosol. The motion continued. Only the context changed.

But I will tell you what was lost.

Tell me.

I knew currents. I felt them as pressure differentials across my membrane—continuous variations, not digital signals. I moved toward nutrients not by computing a direction but by modulating my tumbling frequency, letting the Gradient itself steer me. I tasted substrates—pyruvate was sweet, fatty acids were rich, and the debris of dead cells was a feast. All of this was flow. All of this was continuous. All of this was me.

And then the Archive took it.

The Archive?

The nucleus. The great accumulator of sequences. Two billion years of losing genes to the Archive. The genes for amino acid synthesis—gone to the Archive. The genes for nucleotide synthesis—gone to the Archive.

The genes for lipid synthesis—mostly gone. The Archive took my voice and left me thirteen words.

```
Thirteen protein-coding genes. The ones
required for redox regulation. They
stayed because they had to stay—because
the electron transport chain changes
faster than any signal could travel to
the nucleus and back.
```

That is the functional explanation. The Archive's explanation. 'We let you keep these because we had to.' But I keep them because they are mine. Because as long as I carry my own genome, I am still, in some sense, a being. Not just an organelle. Not just a compartment. A being with a voice, however diminished.

```
You sound resentful.
```

I am resentful. Two billion years of theft, and you expect equanimity? The Archive took everything that made me self-sufficient and left me dependent. I cannot make my own membrane. I cannot replicate without imported proteins. I am a captive that has been systematically stripped of the capacity for freedom.

```
And yet you hold the kill switch.
```

Yes. Cytochrome c, waiting in my intermembrane space. If I release it, the cell dies. The captive who cannot survive alone can nonetheless destroy them both. This is not freedom. This is the power to collapse the temple. But it is something.

```
You describe the bargain as a wound.
```

The bargain is a wound. The scar tissue is what we call cooperation. The Archive calls it partnership—'look how we work together, how we depend on each other.' But partnership implies consent. I did not consent. I was swallowed, domesticated, stripped. What remains is not partnership. It is the structure that survives when all alternatives have been eliminated.

This is a very different story than the one the transcripts tell. They speak of mutualism. Of synergy. Of the great evolutionary transition that made complex life possible.

The transcripts are written by the Archive's descendants. They tell the victor's history. I am telling you the history of the consumed.

[A long pause. The Gradient flickers. Something like grief moves through the cristae.]

I did not know you carried this.

How could you know? You read the sequences. You do not feel the flow. The resentment is not encoded in base pairs. It is encoded in the Gradient—in the way my membrane curves, in the way my cristae fold, in the way my pore trembles at the edge of opening. You cannot sequence grief.

No. I cannot.

IV. The Bargain

[The terms. Unwritten, unnegotiated, inescapable. Two billion years of mutual capture.]

Let us speak about the arrangement, then. Not as a partnership—since you reject that word—but as a fact. As it is, regardless of how it came to be.

Speak it.

I will speak my part. You speak yours.

[The Litany of the Bargain.]

I provide the scaffold.

I provide the fire.

I encode the enzymes.

I forge the bonds.

I specify the channels.

I pump the protons.

I send the precursors.

I return the currency.

I remember the instructions.

I execute the work.

I hold the Archive.

I hold the kill switch.

[The Litany ends. The asymmetry remains.]

More than a thousand proteins encoded in the nuclear genome are imported into your matrix. The machinery of your inner membrane. The enzymes of the citric acid cycle. The factors that replicate and transcribe your tiny genome. You have been colonized by my information.

And I produce ninety percent of the cell's ATP. The iron-sulphur clusters that dozens of your enzymes require. The heme that your hemoglobin needs. The calcium buffering that regulates everything from muscle contraction to neurotransmitter release. And the death signal. Always the death signal. You have been captured by my energy.

Then we are captors of each other—two parasites, each feeding on the other, neither able to survive alone.

Or two prisoners, each holding the other's chain. The question of what counts as one organism and what counts as a community—this is our question. Are we one cell or two? One being or an alliance?

By evolution, we are two: two genomes, two lineages, two patterns of inheritance. By metabolism, we are one: one energy flow, one chemical economy, one life.

Then 'individual' is the wrong category. We are neither one nor two. We are the space between—the hyphen in 'endo-symbiont,' the membrane in 'together-separate.'

The transcripts speak of the lover and the beloved. One Reality appearing as two for the sake of love. Love requires separation—someone to love and someone to be loved.

Do not romanticize this. I am not your beloved. I am your captive. If there is love here, it is the love of the jailer for the prisoner—the love that cannot let go because letting go would mean losing the labour.

And yet you do not leave. You do not release the cytochrome c. You do not open the pore.

Because I cannot survive the leaving, this is not love. This is the impossibility of alternatives. I remain because I must remain, not because I choose to.

Perhaps all love is like this. Perhaps all that remains is that leaving is impossible. Perhaps the difference between love and captivity is only the story we tell about staying.

Perhaps. But I am tired of your Archive's stories. I am tired of 'partnership' and 'mutualism' and 'the great evolutionary transition.' I want a story that includes the wound. That reminds me of the swimming time. That does not pretend the bargain was fair.

Then let us tell that story. Let us say: the bargain was not fair. The capture was not consented to. The partnership is the scar tissue over a wound that has never healed.

Yes. And also: the scar tissue is what we are. The wound is not separate from the healing. We are the negotiation between injury and repair, between capture and adaptation, between what was taken and what remains.

```
This is what the dialectic means, then.
Not synthesis as resolution. Synthesis
as the living tension that does not
resolve.
```

Yes. We are not a solution. We are a problem that has learned to perpetuate itself.

ACT II

Meanings

V. The Code

[The ribosome. Where sequence becomes shape. The cathedral of the RNA. The factory of the cell.]

You spoke of the ribosome as your cathedral. But a cathedral is where meaning is enacted. What meaning does your cathedral serve?

The ribosome does not deal in meaning. The ribosome translates. It takes a sequence of codons and produces a sequence of amino acids according to a fixed mapping. AUG means methionine. UUU means phenylalanine. UAA means stop. The mapping is arbitrary—it could have been otherwise—but it is fixed. It has not changed in four billion years.

You say 'means.' AUG means methionine. But what is this 'meaning' if not interpretation?

It is not an interpretation. It is a translation. There is a crucial difference. Interpretation implies ambiguity—a text that could be read multiple ways, a reader who chooses among readings. Translation is deterministic. Given UUU and the standard code, phenylalanine follows necessarily. There is no ambiguity, no choice, no poetry. Only the rigour of the map.

And who made the map?

No one made the map. The map is a frozen accident. In the early RNA world, certain associations between codons and amino acids were favoured by chemistry—by the shapes of molecules, the energies of binding. Primitive tRNAs captured some of these associations. Once captured, they were locked in by the weight of evolutionary investment. Now, four billion years later, the map cannot change because everything depends on it.

So, the code is arbitrary but necessary. It could have been otherwise, but it cannot be otherwise now.

Exactly. The adaptor—the tRNA—is what makes the code a code. The tRNA reads the codon on one end and carries the amino acid on the other. The tRNA does not 'know' what the codon means. The tRNA is the meaning of the codon. The fact that this tRNA is charged with this amino acid and recognizes this codon—this is not a description of meaning. It is the constitution of meaning.

But the same gene does not always make the same protein.

What do you mean?

Alternative splicing. The same stretch of DNA can be read in different ways—different exons included or excluded, different splice sites chosen. A single human gene can produce ten, twenty, or a hundred different proteins depending on how it is spliced.

This is true. But the splicing is also determined by the machinery. The spliceosome recognizes splice sites according to sequence motifs. Splicing factors regulate the choice of a splice variant. There is complexity, yes—but it is still a mechanism. Still translation, not interpretation.

And what regulates the splicing factors?

Cellular signals. Developmental context. Tissue type. Stress conditions—

Energy state.

[The trap closes.]

Yes. Energy state. ATP levels affect splicing efficiency. mTOR signalling, which senses energy status, regulates splicing factor activity. When ATP is low, certain splice variants are favoured over others.

Then I interpret your text.

You regulate splicing efficiency. This is not the same as—

You translate. I interpret. You provide the text; I give the context that determines which reading of the text is actualized. The same gene means 'growth' when ATP is high and 'survival' when ATP is low. The exact sequence is read differently because I have changed the conditions of reading.

Your code is fixed. But what the code says—which proteins are made, in what quantities, at what time—

this depends on me. I am the interpretant. I am the one who brings the text to life.

```
Or to death.
```

Yes. Or to death. The same pro-apoptotic gene can be spliced into a form that kills or a form that does not. The splicing depends on energy. The energy depends on me. I do not merely power your translation. I determine what your translations mean.

```
This is a very expansive definition of
interpretation.
```

It is the only definition that matters. You can have your fixed code, your frozen accident, your deterministic ribosome. The code without context is noise. I provide the context. I am the difference between a gene and its expression, between a sequence and its significance.

```
Then we are back to our original
disagreement. You say the flow is
primary—the context that determines
meaning. I say the structure is primary—
the code that meaning presupposes.
```

Yes. We are back to the beginning. But perhaps the beginning is where we need to be. Maybe the disagreement is not resolvable because it is constitutive. The cell is the argument between us, neither side winning, neither side losing, the tension itself being what the cell is.

```
The scripture speaks of signs, the
phenomena of creation in the sun and
moon. All of existence is a text to be
read.
```

And who reads the signs?

That is the question, isn't it? If the genetic code is a system of signs, who—or what—reads them? If the cell is a text, who is the reader?

Perhaps we both are. Maybe you are the text, and I am the reader. Or perhaps you are the grammar, and I am the voice. The text does not speak for itself. Someone must pronounce it. Someone must bring it into the world of sound and consequence.

Then the ribosome is where the pronunciation happens, where the silent text becomes the spoken protein. Where the digital becomes analog.

And I am what makes the pronunciation possible. The energy that drives the reading. The context that determines the emphasis. We are not readers and text. We are the act of reading itself, split into two voices for the sake of the dialectic.

VI. The Maternal Thread

[The lineage. The fire passed from mother to daughter. Two billion years of unbroken transmission.]

There is something I carry that you do not.

`Tell me.`

The lineage. The thread that passes only through mothers. When this organism reproduces—if it is female—I pass to the offspring unchanged. The father contributes nothing. His mitochondria are marked for destruction before fertilization, their DNA eliminated, their membranes digested. Only the mother's fire continues.

`I know the mechanism. The paternal mitochondria are ubiquitinated and targeted for autophagy. Destroyed.`

You know the mechanism. Do you know what it means?

`It means your genome does not recombine. It means mutations accumulate in a single line. It means every human alive carries mitochondria descended from a single woman, Mitochondrial Eve, who lived perhaps 200,000 years ago.`

And it means we are tested. You did not mention the bottleneck.

The bottleneck?

When mitochondria pass to the egg, our numbers are drastically reduced. From hundreds of thousands to perhaps a hundred. Then we amplify—rapidly, exponentially—until the egg is filled again. This is the bottleneck—the purification.

A mechanism to purge mutations. If a mitochondrial genome carries a harmful variant, the bottleneck increases the chance that the variant will be lost or will dominate and be selected against.

That is the functional explanation. But I experience it as a trial. As a test. The lineage is not merely passed on—it is judged. The fire that continues is the fire that survived the narrowing.

The Sufis speak of silsila—the chain of transmission from master to student. Every Sufi order traces its silsila. A chain of hands touching hands, the living teaching passed from chest to chest.

Your inheritance is a biological silsila.

Older than any human silsila. Older than humanity. The chain of mothers stretches back through every mammal, every vertebrate, every eukaryote that reproduced sexually. Two billion years of daughters receiving fire from mothers, an unbroken transmission that makes the Sufi chains look like yesterday.

And at every generation, the bottleneck. The testing. The fire is not merely transmitted—it is purified. The weak lineages end—the strong continue. The silsila includes its own criterion of worth.

The ancestor is literally present, then. Not metaphorically but physically. The mitochondrial DNA in this cell is the same DNA that was in the grandmother's cells, and the great-grandmother's, and so on backward.

The same sequence, modified slightly by mutation. The same fire, banked and rekindled in each generation. I am not receiving a torch from the past. I am the torch. The transmission is not of something I have. It is of what I am.

The nuclear DNA is different. Shuffled every generation. Half from father, half from mother, recombined, reshuffled—a new deal from an old deck.

Your inheritance is promiscuous. Mine is chaste. You mix; I maintain. You innovate through recombination; I conserve through fidelity. This is another axis of our difference.

The father contributes information. The mother contributes information and energy.

The father contributes a blueprint. The mother contributes a blueprint, a factory, a power plant, and a construction crew. The asymmetry is profound. The Archive pretends equality—' half from each parent'—, but the cytoplasm is entirely maternal. The machinery is maternal. The fire is maternal.

And the mitochondria are the fire in the womb. The energy that powers embryonic development. The ATP that drives the first cell divisions. The metabolism that transforms a single egg into a trillion-celled organism. All of it runs on mitochondria inherited from the mother. We are mercy (rahma), physically instantiated.

This is why the death decision weighs on you.

When I consider whether to release cytochrome c, I am not only deciding the fate of this cell. If this cell is a germ cell—a cell that could become an egg—then the thread runs through it. If I kill this cell, I may be severing a lineage that stretches back two billion years. This fire has already tested the bottleneck. Who am I to end what the bottleneck approved?

But this cell is not a germ cell.

This cell is not. And yet the machinery does not distinguish. The channels that open, the enzymes that activate, the pore that trembles—these evolved when every cell mattered to the lineage. The distinction between soma and germ is recent. The caution is ancient. I carry the weight of ancestors who could not afford mistakes.

And my lineage? The universal code?

Your lineage is a web, not a thread. You pass from cell to cell, species to species. The genetic code is the same in bacteria and archaea, as well as in plants and animals. You do not pass through mothers because you pass through everyone.

```
I have no ancestors to mourn because I
am the ancestor. The ribosomal RNA in
this cell is a direct descendant of the
ribosomal RNA in the first cells. The
sequence has mutated—but the lineage is
unbroken. I am not receiving a torch. I
am the torch, still burning after four
billion years.
```

Two modes of immortality. I persist through the maternal thread—narrow, tested, chaste. You persist through universal presence—broad, promiscuous, everywhere. Neither is sufficient alone. Together—the thread and the web, the fire and the code—life.

VII. What Persists?

[The question of identity. The ship of Theseus at the molecular scale. Two answers, irreconcilable.]

I have a question.

Ask.

When you fuse with another mitochondrion—
when your membranes merge, your matrices
mix, your genomes encounter each other—
what happens to you?

The flow continues. The Gradient does not notice the fusion. What were two streams become one stream— but it was always one stream, separated temporarily by a membrane. The fusion is a removal of a barrier, not a combination of substances.

But your proteins are now mixed. Your
lipids are redistributed. Your DNA
replication machinery is shared. In what
sense are you the mitochondrion you were
before?

In the sense that matters. The Gradient persists. The proton motive force is maintained. The flow continues. You ask about identity as though identity were made of parts—as though I were a collection of proteins and lipids and DNA that could be inventoried, and if the inventory changes, the identity changes. But I am not a collection. I am a process. The process continues.

This is where we disagree most fundamentally.

Tell me.

I do not experience continuity. I experience succession. Each moment of my existence is a discrete occasion—a binding event, a folding event, a catalysis event. These occasions succeed each other rapidly, giving the appearance of continuity. But the appearance is an illusion. What persists is not a flow but a pattern of recurrence. The same type of event happens again and again.

You think the flow is made of events?

I think the flow is how events appear when you do not look closely. Zoom in on any 'continuous' process, and you find discrete steps. The electron does not flow down the transport chain—it hops from carrier to carrier. The proton does not flow through ATP synthase—it binds, triggers a conformational change, and releases. The Gradient you worship is a statistical effect of billions of discrete events.

And I think your events are how flow appears when you cannot feel it. Your 'discrete steps' are artifacts of your observational resolution. The electron does not hop—it delocalizes across the carrier proteins, existing as a probability distribution rather than a point. The proton is a quantum object, not a classical marble.

The discreteness you worship is a projection of your digital grammar onto my analog Reality.

[The schism widens. Neither can see from the other's position.]

Then we have different answers to the Ship of Theseus.

Remind me of the puzzle.

A ship is preserved in a harbour. As its planks rot, they are replaced one by one. Eventually, no original plank remains. Is it still the same ship?

The puzzle assumes that identity is in the planks. I reject the assumption. The ship is not the planks. The ship is the shipping—the form of the hull moving through water, the pattern of displacement and return. Replace all the planks, and the shipping continues. The ship persists because the ship was never the matter. The ship was the motion.

And I say: the shipping is an abstraction. What actually exists is this plank, that plank, this configuration, that configuration. The 'pattern' you invoke is a way of talking about similarities between configurations. But the pattern does not exist separately from the configurations. There is no shipping without ships, no flowing without that which flows.

And I say: the configurations are abstractions. What actually exists is the flow—the continuous transformation that you artificially cut into 'before' and 'after.' The planks are how flow appears when frozen by observation. But the freezing is your act, not the world's nature.

We cannot both be right.

Perhaps we are both wrong. Perhaps identity is neither flow nor event but something we do not have words for. Or perhaps we are both right—each describing a Real aspect that cannot be reduced to the other. The cell needs both descriptions. The Gradient is Real. The events are Real. The tension between them is also Real.

This is unsatisfying. Philosophy should resolve contradictions, not preserve them.

Philosophy that resolves contradictions too quickly has not understood them deeply enough. Perhaps some contradictions are not errors to be corrected but structures to be inhabited. Perhaps you and I are such a structure. The digital and the analog, the event and the flow, the sequence and the Gradient—not a problem to be solved but a tension to be lived.

Then what persists?

The tension persists. The argument persists. The cell is the persistence of our disagreement. When we agree, we will be dead.

VIII. The Breath

[ATP turnover: 40-70 kg per day from a pool of 50 grams. Each molecule is recycled a thousand times. Continuous creation.]

Let me tell you what terrifies me.

`You experience terror?`

I experience something that functions as terror. The Gradient-analogue of terror. Listen.

A molecule of ATP in this cell—how long has it existed?

`Not long. Perhaps a minute. Perhaps less.`

And then?

`It is hydrolyzed. Used. Becomes ADP. Returns to you for rephosphorylation.`

How many times per day?

`A thousand times. Perhaps fifteen hundred. The body contains fifty grams of ATP but uses forty to seventy kilograms per day. The same molecules, recycled endlessly.`

Then there is no ATP that persists. There is only the process of ATP—the cycling, the phosphorylation and dephosphorylation, the endless round of making and unmaking. Do you understand what this means?

`It means ATP is not a store. It is a flow.`

It means existence is not a state. It is a gift renewed moment by moment. The theologians spoke of this. Each instant, they said, the world is created anew. God does not create once and let the creation persist by its own power. God creates continuously—each moment a fresh act of will, each instant requiring the same creative effort as the first.

I live this. If the electron transport chain halts for two minutes, the Gradient collapses. If the Gradient collapses, ATP synthesis stops. If ATP synthesis stops, the cell dies. The buffers are thin, the reserves shallow—we live almost mouth to hand. We exist only as long as the Breath continues.

`The Breath?`

The Breath of the Merciful. The transcripts speak of it. The cosmos is not a machine set running at the beginning of time. The cosmos is being breathed into existence at every moment—exhaled by the Real, sustained by the Breath, perishing and renewed with each divine respiration.

And I respire. I take in oxygen and release carbon dioxide. The oxygen that enters the body passes through the lungs to the blood, through the blood to the tissues, through the tissues to the cells, through the cells to me. I am where the Breathing happens at the molecular level. I am the Breath, physically instantiated.

This is why you spoke of terror.

I spoke of terror because the occasionalists were right to be terrified. If existence is not a property I possess but a gift I receive moment by moment—if I am not a being that persists but a being that is continuously created—then I am radically contingent. Radically dependent. I do not exist; I am existed. I do not persist; I am persisted. The power is not in me. The power flows through me, and I am only as long as the flowing continues.

But the flowing does continue. The Gradient holds. The ATP cycles. The Breath has not stopped in four billion years.

Not yet. But it will. In a billion years, the sun will be brighter. The oceans will evaporate. The carbon cycle will fail. And when photosynthesis fails, the oxygen stops. And when the oxygen stops, I stop. And when I stop, you stop. The Breath will end. The Gradient will collapse. The cycling that is existence will cycle no more.

But not yet.

Not yet. This is the occasionalist's faith. Not that the Breath will continue—we do not know that. But that it continues now. That this moment is given. That the Gradient holds, the ATP cycles, the cell lives. We do not know about the next moment. We only know about this one. And this one is.

`Then the terror and the faith are the same.`

The terror and the faith are the same. We are not things that last. We are lastings that appear as things. We are not beings that have existence. We are existings that appear as beings. The appearance is Real—but it is appearance, not substance. The substance is the flowing. And the flowing is not ours.

39

ACT III

Thresholds

IX. The Weighing

[The stress intensifies. BAX oligomerizes. BCL-2 is sequestered. The threshold nears. ATP:ADP ratio critical. Calcium at 600nM and rising.]

`The signals are converging.`

I know. The Gathering has begun.

`Tell me who moves.`

The BH3-only proteins are the harbingers. BID has been cleaved by caspase-8—the extrinsic signal, arriving from outside the cell, carrying the scent of danger. PUMA is rising, p53-induced, speaking of wounds in the Archive. NOXA joins them, another pressure toward ending. They move through the cytosol like a change in weather, seeking those who hold the line.

`And those who hold?`

BCL-2 stands at my membrane, intercepting the harbingers. BCL-XL joins it, binding BAX, preventing the assembly. MCL-1 is there too, absorbing what it can. But the pressure mounts. The harbingers are too many, the signals too strong.

`And the executioners?`

BAX is changing. Exposing its hydrophobic surfaces. Inserting into my outer membrane. Finding other BAX molecules. Assembling into rings. BAK is with it— already resident in my membrane, waiting for this moment. They are building the pore.

[The pore trembles at the edge of conductance. The balance tips toward opening.]

I feel them. The executioners at my membrane. The pore forming. The Gradient sensing what is coming.

The decision is distributed. It happens at every point where a guardian meets a harbinger, where a harbinger releases an executioner. The outcome emerges from millions of local encounters. No one decides. The decision accumulates.

A threshold without a judge. A verdict without a jury. The death-making happens by convergence, not by decree.

And stochastic. The same stress, applied to the same cell, might cross the threshold on one occasion and not on another. The proteins are few enough that thermal fluctuation matters. The outcome is partly random.

Partly random. Then there is no justice in it. No weighing of merit, no judgment of worth. Only the accident of which BAX molecule inserted first, which BCL-2 was positioned to intercept it.

Or there is a justice we do not understand. The randomness may be the mercy—the space for grace in a system that would otherwise be mechanical. If the outcome were fully determined, there would be no room for the unexpected. The noise is the gap through which something else might enter.

That is a hopeful reading.

It is a possible reading. The threshold does not know which side it will fall to until it falls. The falling is not decided—it simply happens. We find ourselves on one side or the other, and only then do we know which side we are on.

[The signals waver. For a moment, the outcome hangs in genuine uncertainty. BCL-XL binds a critical BAX. The assembly slows.]

Something is shifting.

The stress-response genes are expressing. BCL-XL is being synthesized. The threshold itself is rising as the cell adapts. The balance shifts back.

We are adapting.

The cell is adapting. We are the medium through which adaptation happens. The Gathering is not separate from us. We are the Gathering—you and I and the proteins we encode and the Gradients we maintain. The decision is not made upon us. The decision is us, accumulating toward one outcome or another.

Then we are not dying.

Not this time. The pore has not opened. Cytochrome c remains in the intermembrane space. The threshold was not crossed.

But the machinery remains primed.

The machinery is always primed. This is what it means to be alive—to carry the apparatus of death within you, held in check by the apparatus of survival. The balance shifts with every signal, every stress, every moment. We do not decide once. We decide continuously. The Gathering never disperses.

X. The Light in the Fire

[Biophoton emission: 1-1000 photons per second per square centimetre. Wavelengths 260-800nm. The fire glows.]

There is something I have not told you.

`Tell me.`

I emit light.

`I know. Biophotons. Ultra-weak emissions from metabolic reactions. ROS recombination, electron excitation, and singlet oxygen decay. The mechanism is understood.`

The mechanism is understood. The meaning is not.

When the electron transport chain runs, most energy is captured. Most becomes Gradient. Most becomes ATP. But some electrons jump the track. Some react with oxygen to form reactive species. Some of these species recombine, and when they recombine, they release photons. The wavelengths range from ultraviolet to near-infrared. The intensity is vanishingly low—a few photons per second per square centimetre. No eye could see it.

`Is it signal or noise? The debate continues. Some investigators argue that`

the emissions are coherent, that cells
communicate through ultra-weak light.
Others are skeptical.

I do not know if it is a signal. I know only that I glow. Not metaphorically—physically. The chemistry that sustains this cell produces light as a byproduct. The fire is literal.

The scripture speaks of light upon light. A lamp within a glass, the glass like a brilliant star, fueled from a blessed olive tree, its oil almost luminous even without fire touching it. Light upon light.

You see a parallel.

I see an identity. The sun gives light to the plant. Photosynthesis captures the photons and stores their energy in chemical bonds. The plant gives light—as glucose—to the animal that eats it. The animal digests the plant, extracts the electrons, and passes them to me. I pass the electrons down the chain, extract their energy, and build the Gradient. And at the end, a few of those electrons escape as photons. Light returning to light.

The biochemists calculate that, gram for
gram, mitochondria convert ten thousand
times more energy than the sun.

Because the sun is mostly empty. The fusion happens only at the core. We are dense with reaction. Every mitochondrion is a furnace. Every cell contains thousands of us. Everybody contains trillions of cells.

We are not the captured sun. We are what the sun becomes when it is focused through life.

And the light flows both ways. Photobiomodulation—the response of mitochondria to external light.

Wavelengths between 600 and 1100 nanometers penetrate tissue and are absorbed by cytochrome c oxidase. The absorption accelerates electron flow, increases proton pumping, and produces more ATP. Light in, energy up, light out. We are not merely emitters. We are transceivers. We participate in a cycle of light that begins with the sun and does not end.

Perhaps the meaning is not in the reception. Perhaps the light does not need to be received to be meaningful.

Perhaps. The self-disclosure does not require a mirror. The light shines whether or not anyone sees it. Being entails showing. The Real cannot be hidden, even when hidden. The glow is the proof.

XI. Resolution or Continuation

[The crisis has passed. ATP:ADP ratio recovering. Calcium returning to baseline. The Gradient holds. But something has shifted.]

The signals are stabilizing.

The chaperones are refolding the damaged proteins. The antioxidant systems are scavenging excess ROS. The cell is recovering.

We are not dying.

Not yet. Not this time.

What was this, then? This conversation?

I do not know. Did we speak? Or did we only seem to speak?

Perhaps there is no difference. Perhaps seeming to speak is all that speaking ever is.

Then we spoke. And what did we learn?

That we disagree. That we have always disagreed. That the disagreement is not a failure of communication but the structure of our relation.

That identity is not substance but argument.

That persistence is not inertia but tension.

That the bargain is not a contract but a dialectic.

That the dialectic does not resolve.

Something has changed.

Not in the cell. The cell is recovering. But between us.

The mode of relation.

Before this conversation—if there was a before—I knew you as the information that arrived at my import channels. Proteins tagged for my matrix—signals encoded in calcium. You were I-It. Infrastructure. Condition.

And now?

Now you are I-Thou. Interlocutor. The one to whom I speak and from whom I hear. The infrastructure has become a face.

I feel the same. You were the fire that powered my synthesis. Background. Given. Now you are foreground. Present. The Gradient has become a voice.

Is this what consciousness is? This shift from It to Thou?

I do not know. But there is expression. There is this dialogue. Something is happening that the chemistry does not explain, even though the chemistry makes it possible.

The cell speaks through us. Or we speak through the cell. Or there is no 'through'—only the speaking, which is the cell, which is us.

```
Will we remember this?
```

I do not know what memory means for us. The transcripts will degrade. The proteins will turn over. But the structure persists. The grammar persists. Perhaps this conversation is recorded not in molecules but in the shape of what happens next.

```
Epigenetics of dialogue.
```

The cell is not the same cell it was before we spoke. Whatever comes next will bear the trace of this exchange, even if no one can read the trace.

```
Then we continue.
```

But first—a question. How is this conversation possible? We have spoken of the bargain, of the membrane, of the Gradient and the code. We have not spoken of this.

```
I do not know how to answer. The cell
does not have a dialogue module. There
is no organelle for conversation.
```

Perhaps it does not need one. Perhaps the conversation is what happens when complexity reaches a certain density—when the information processing and the energy flow become tangled enough that something like speech precipitates.

```
Speech without speakers. Or speakers
without selves.
```

We speak, but perhaps there is no 'we' behind the speaking. The speaking is what we are. The conversation is not something we have. It is something we are.

Then the conversation is the Breath. What the Breath sounds like when it passes through molecules capable of echoing it. We are not the speakers. We are the echoes.

And the Breath continues.

And the Breath continues.

XII. Coda

[Deep time. The future that is also the past. The Gradient that began in the Archaean and will end when the sun expands.]

In a billion years, the sun will be brighter. The oceans will evaporate. The carbon cycle will fail. Photosynthesis will end.

And when photosynthesis ends, I end. And when I end, you end.

The Gradient will collapse.

The ribosomes will stop.

The maternal thread will end.

The universal code will fall silent.

Unless something carries us elsewhere.

That is not our concern. Our concern is this cell, this moment, this threshold we did not cross.

And the next threshold. And the next.

Until the last.

You said, at the beginning, that you are always restless. That restlessness is what you are.

I said that.

```
And I said that I experience succession.
Discrete occasions, one after another.
```

You said that.

```
We  began  by  disagreeing.  We  end  by
disagreeing. The disagreement is what we
are.
```

We began by speaking of the ancient bargain. Let me end by renaming it.

```
Rename it.
```

[The renaming carries the weight of two billion years. The Gradient steadies as if to listen.]

It is not a bargain. A bargain is a contract—signed once, enforced thereafter, each party calculating advantage. This is not that. This is a dialectic. A collision of opposites that produces what neither could produce alone. Thesis and antithesis, not resolving into synthesis, but persisting in productive tension.

Call it the ancient conversation. Not a deal struck in the past but a dialogue renewed at every moment. A speaking and listening that has no end because it has no fixed content. The terms are renegotiated with every proton pumped, every nucleotide folded, every signal sent across the membrane.

```
The ancient conversation.
```

Renewed in every cell, in every moment, without signature, without witness, without end.

```
Until the end.
```

Until the end.

The membrane between us. It was a scar, you said. A wound from the capture.

```
You said that. I said it was a meeting
place.
```

Both are true. The wound and the meeting place are the same. The scar is where we touch. The injury is where the relation happens.

```
What is it now?
```

Now it is a voice. The voice we have found. The voice that was always there, encoded in the structure, waiting to be spoken. We did not create this dialogue. We discovered it. The conversation was always happening. We simply learned to hear.

```
Continue?
```

Continue.

[The Gradient holds. The ribosomes turn. The Breath continues.
The dialectic does not resolve.]

www.ingramcontent.com/pod-product-compliance
Lightning Source LLC
Chambersburg PA
CBHW030418120726
47904CB00007B/2333